Gramma's glasses

written by
William A. Guiffré

illustrated by
Barbara Pippin

Coastal Publishing, Inc.
504 Amberjack Way
Summerville, SC 29485
843-821-6168
www.coastalpublishingbooks.com
coastalpublishing@earthlink.net

Cataloging-in-Publication Data

Guiffré, William, 1934 -

Gramma's Glasses / by William Guiffré ; illustrated by Barbara Pippin
p. cm.
SUMMARY: When Gramma loses her glasses, her grandchildren suggest many unusual places
where they might be, from a rainbow in the sky to inside the oven.

ISBN - 1-931650-19-5 - HB
ISBN - 1-931650-35-7 - PB

[1. Eyeglasses -- Fiction. 2. Lost and found possessions -- Fiction. 3. Grandmothers -- Fiction.
4. Stories in rhyme.] I. Pippin, Barbara. ill. II. Title.
PZ8.3.G947Gr 998
[E]--dc21

Printed and bound in the United States of America

The school children absolutely loved Gramma's Glasses, a delightful, amusing, interesting story that ha
appeal to the young child and to the parent. Illustrations embellish the story in a compatible context. As an elemen
tary consultant, I would recommend this book as part of classroom libraries. I can visualize this book being read ove
and over again. Congratulations!
Constance T. Hall, Reading Specialist/Consultant, Board of Education, Norwalk, Connecticut.

A delightful book! I am anxious for our preschool story hour to begin this fall so I can read the book to ou
children here in Marion, a warm and cuddly book for children.
Pam Wolfanger, Library Manager, Marion, New York Public Library.

I found the story not only one that young people enjoy and relate to but also one that covers several instruc
tional levels and concepts. The illustrations are delightful! I am anxiously awaiting your next book.
Barbara Kidd, Coordinator of Federal Programs, Troy City School District

Captures the true joy and treasure of the relationship between grandma and her grandchildren. It is a treasure
untouched by the hustle and bustle of our world but rather by sensitivity and spontaneity and true love. I think every
grandma should own it.
Nancy Johnstone, Teacher Multi-age K-2 Hilton central School District, Hilton, NY.

Simply delightful! What a wonderful children's story with a subject we can all relate to-finding our glasses
Loved the creative locations for the missing spectacles, the clever rhyming lines and the heartwarming illustrations
Great Story book!
Melony Sabo Bradley, English teacher Hilton Head, SC.

William A. Guiffré was born in Brooklyn, N.Y. in 1934 and lived in Vermont, Maryland and Virginia before attending the University of Rochester in New York on a Navy Scholarship. After graduating with a BA in English, he married Ann Kelley of Brighton, N.Y. and served three years as an officer in the US Navy.

He began his education career at the Twelve Corners Middle School in Brighton, N.Y. teaching English to 7th and 8th graders. After earning his Masters degree in counseling at the U of R, he continued as guidance counselor at the school until he completed his studies for the Doctorate Degree in Educational Administration also at the University of Rochester.

His career then took him to Rush Henrietta, New York where he served for two years as the Administrative Assistant to the Superintendent of Schools.

After a year as Assistant Principal of Webster Schroeder High School, Dr. Guiffré became principal of the Victor Senior High School where he served for 15 years until his retirement. Guiffré was very active both professionally and as a community member serving in several organizations in leadership roles locally and at regional and state levels. Following retirement he was elected to the Victor School Board where he served until he and his wife sold their home of 34 years and became summer residents of Inlet, N.Y. and winter residents of Kiawah Island, S.C.

It was during retirement that Guiffré began writing children's picture books. He first became associated with Coastal Publishing when his second and third books were selected for publication by Coastal. His extensive background in education and his efforts in the marketing of his own books make him uniquely qualified to serve the needs of Coastal publishing and its authors. He will bring his talents not only to sales and marketing but also to selection and editing of new books. Coastal Publishing, Inc. welcomes him to the staff.

Dedication

Dedicated to our 23 grandchildren.

Where are Gramma's glasses?
Heaven only knows!
The last time Gramma saw them
They were sitting on her nose.

"I know," offered Hannah,
With a twinkle in her eye,
"They're sliding on a rainbow
Away up in the sky."

"They were," agreed Breanna,
Nodding wisely as could be,
"But they slid right off that rainbow
And settled in a tree."

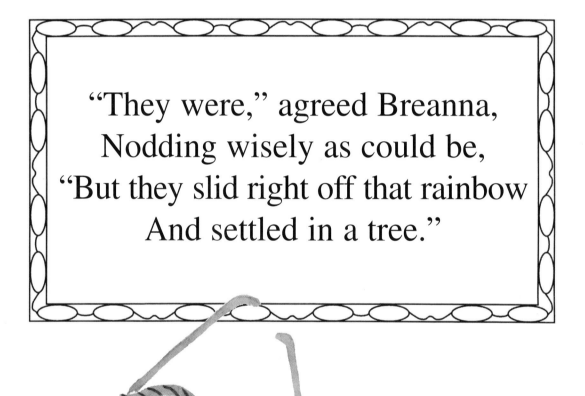

"George saw them too,"
Kidded Robby like the rest.
"They landed on a robin
Who's sitting on her nest."

"No way!" answered Tyler,
Eating ice cream from his dish,

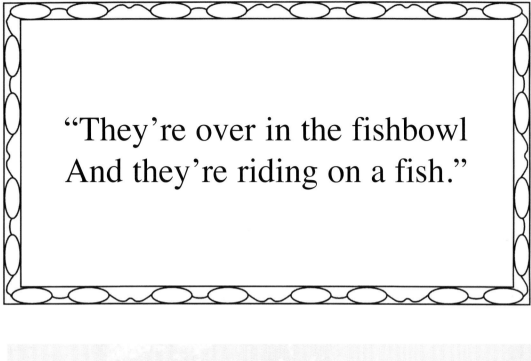

"They're over in the fishbowl
And they're riding on a fish."

"They're not!" exclaimed Rebecca,
With hands upon her hips,
"You left them in the cupboard
Next to a bag of chips."

"Not so!" chimed in Machias,
His nose behind his book,
"You left them in the bathtub!
Why don't we go and look?"

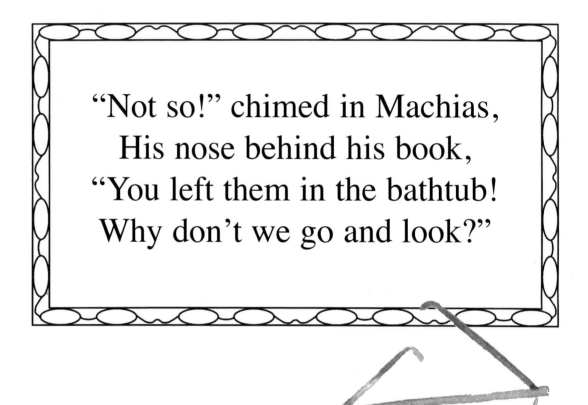

"You're teasing me, aren't you,
You silly little scamps?
Get serious and tell me
Before I go ask Gramps."

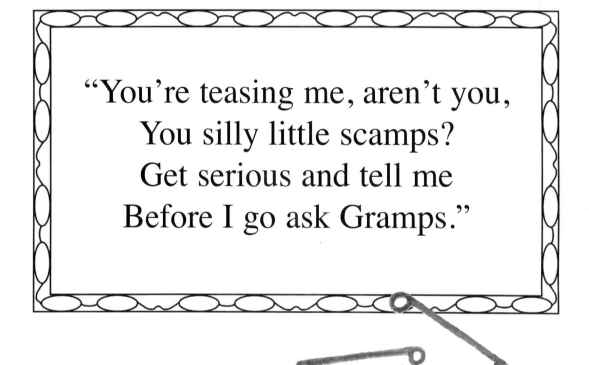

"O.K.!" offered Nolan,
Taking clues from his cousin,
"I saw them just this morning
When you left them in the oven."

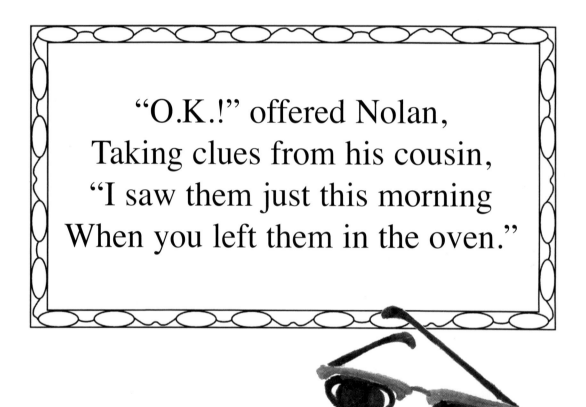

"That's true," nodded Matthew,
as he gave them all a wink,
"Or were they in the dishpan
Over there in the sink?"

"Let's search and find them,"
Offered Gabrielle to all.
"We'll look in the bedroom,
Gramma, and you look
in the hall."

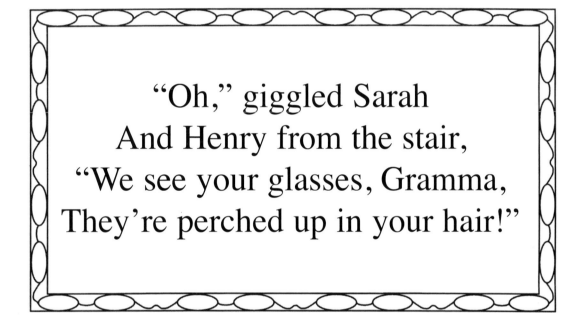

"Oh," giggled Sarah
And Henry from the stair,
"We see your glasses, Gramma,
They're perched up in your hair!"

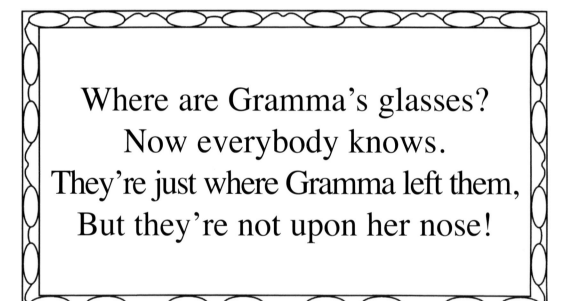

Where are Gramma's glasses?
Now everybody knows.
They're just where Gramma left them,
But they're not upon her nose!

Other titles written by
William A. Guiffré:

The First Gift of Christmas
The Wrong Side of the Bed
Angelita's Song